cuillère kweeáir

verre d'eau vayr do

crêpe krep

6 *six* seece

7 *sept* set

8 *huit* weet

9 *neuf* nurf

10 *dix* deece

glace glass

pomme pom

croissant krwassón

avion aveeón

Toto in Paris

BIDDY STREVENS

A first taste of France for young children

LITTLE, BROWN

Boston · Toronto · London

For Thomas and all his friends

Illustrations and text copyright © 1991 by Bridget Strevens Romer
First published in Great Britain in 1991 by Little, Brown and Company (UK) Limited
Beacon House, 30 North End Road, London W14 0SH

Designed by Janet James
Typeset by DP Photosetting, Aylesbury, Bucks
Printed and bound in Belgium by Proost, Turnhout

A CIP catalogue record for this book is available from the British Library
ISBN 0-316-88868-0

Toto and his parents have just arrived in Paris.

"I'll take you up to Sylvie's apartment. Hurry up now! Our taxi is waiting."

Toto's father presses the button on the intercom.

"Have a great day!" says Toto's mother, giving him a big hug.

"*Bonjour, Messieurs!*" says a lady cleaning the floor.

"Go on Toto, say '*Bonjour Madame*' to the *concierge*!" Toto's father insists.

"*Excusez-moi!* That's all the French I know." Toto replies, climbing the stairs.

"Are we almost there? Will you carry my plane, Dad?"

"Fourth floor on the right. Here we are at last!" says Toto's father.
"May I ring the bell?" Toto asks.

"*Bonjour* Toto!" says Sylvie, kissing him on each cheek. Paulette kisses him twice too.
"Woof!" says Mimi in dog language.
"See you later, Toto!" Toto's father waves at them.
"*A bientôt!*"

"Come and have breakfast!" says Sylvie, sitting down at the table, "*du pain* – just how I like it!" Sylvie dips some bread into her *chocolat chaud*.

"Wow, I've never seen such a big bowl of hot chocolate!" Toto whistles, "and a *croissant* and jam, yummy!"

"Oh no! Paulette, look what Mimi's doing!"

Now Mimi can't speak French or
English, but you can tell she wants to
go out for a walk.

"Wait for us Mimi!", they all shout
as she races down the stairs and out into
the street.

"*Vite, vite!* Hurry! Come back Mimi!", they all cry as she runs into the busy boulevard. "Stop that dog!"

Mimi runs twice around a hot chestnut stall and through the legs of a man sweeping the street.

"Ça alors!" he says, which simply means "Well I never!"

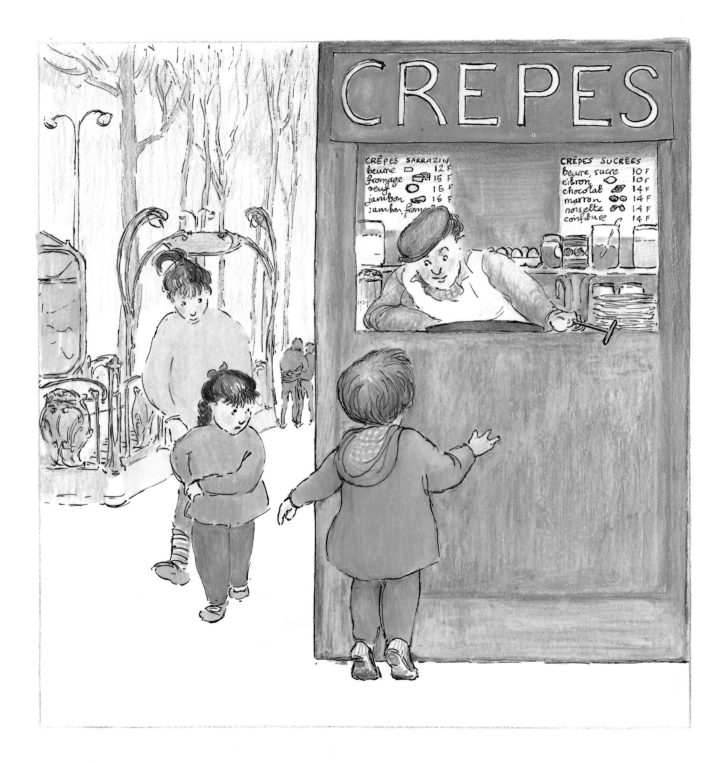

"*Excusez-moi!*" Toto interrupts a man making pancakes, "Did you see a dog run past here?"

"*Oui, par là!* That way!" the man points.

"*Aie, aie, aie*", Sylvie wails, "I've got a stitch from running too fast!"

Outside a pet shop Mimi suddenly screeches to a halt. What is this? Someone is standing on her lead!

"*Un chien! Ça alors!*" the pet shop owner says to himself. "My lucky day!"

"*Ça alors!*" cries a parrot peering over his shoulder.

"Mimi can't be far now," Toto thinks to himself.

"*Excusez-moi!*", he addresses a man standing on one leg outside a pet shop, "Did you see a dog run past here?"

"*Un chien? Non!*", the man shakes his head slowly. But then he points and says "*. . . Oui. Par là!*"

Toto has no idea what the man is doing with his other leg. Mimi finds herself in a cage with some white mice. Poor Mimi! She doesn't know what to say to them. She can't speak Mouse.

"What a beautiful dog! André, wait!" a lady orders her *chauffeur*.

"Aren't you sweet!" she tells Mimi.

"That's funny", says the pet shop owner, "you look just like that singer, what's-her-name . . . Sophie Starlette".

"But I AM Sophie Starlette", the lady says grandly, "now tell me, *Monsieur*, how much is that dog?"

"*Ce chien, Madame?* Very special," he sniffs, "very expensive, but worth every *centime*. Ten thousand francs!"

By lunchtime, Toto, Sylvie and Paulette are halfway up the *Avenue de l'Opera*.

"It's no use looking any more! We've lost her forever!" Paulette bursts into tears.

"Where can you be Mimi? Please come back, wherever you are, I miss you already", Sylvie whispers to herself.

"Don't worry, I'm sure we'll find her somehow", Toto comforts them.

Mimi looks around – something tells
her nose that her old friends are nearby.
The traffic light turns red and – off she
goes!

"*Mon chien, au secours,* help!" Sophie
Starlette shouts and waves her arms
about.

"Mimi, you're back!" Paulette cries,
"It's a miracle!"
Mimi licks everyone on both cheeks
and wags her tail.
"But what happened? How did you
get here?" Toto wonders.

"That's MY dog, I bought it this morning!" cries Sophie Starlette. What a commotion! Everyone shouts and waves their arms about.

"It's a SHE!" "She belongs to US!"

"Woof! Woof!", reply Toto, Sylvie and Mimi.

"*S'il vous plaît*," a *gendarme* appears and raises his hands.

"IF YOU PLEASE, ONE story at a time! . . .

What has the dog to say for itself?"

"Look!" Toto points, "she wants us to follow her!"

Toto holds Mimi's lead as tight as he can and sets off, with a very disgruntled procession in his wake.

"But this is where I bought my dog this morning!" cries Sophie Starlette ". . . and that's the man who sold him to me!"

"He's running away! Quick, let's get him Mimi!" Toto shouts. All the pets start squeaking, mewing, barking, whistling and cawing in a hundred and one different languages. "*Par là, par là*", the parrot screeches.

"After him Mimi, *vite, vite!*" Toto shouts.

"*Attention!*" a fruit seller cries out. "Look where you're going!"
Too late, there are apples all over the place.

"*Excusez-moi!*" Toto calls back though it's not his fault.
Suddenly the villain disappears into a shop.

"André, take a picture of us all!", Sophie Starlette orders her *chauffeur*. She kisses everyone on each cheek.

"Darling Mimi, thanks to you I won't feel so lonely. You must come and visit me, with all your friends, and we'll go out for some wonderful walks together, won't we?"

"Oh, please don't talk about walking!" groans Sylvie. "*J'ai faim!*"

"I'm famished too!" "Woof, WOOF!" Toto and Mimi agree.

"We didn't have lunch!" Paulette explains.

"No lunch?", cries Sophie, "Well then, let me take you all to a *café* for a big treat!"

"*Bon appetit!*" says Sophie. She orders them huge *sandwiches mixtes*, followed by *petits pains au chocolat* and *tarte aux pommes*.

The *garçon* brings them a final treat.

"*Une glace à la fraise! Merci beaucoup!*" says Sylvie.

"Thank you . . ." says Toto, "*merci!* Strawberry ice cream – my favourite! This drink is yummy too."

"It's called *grenadine*" Sophie tells him, "but I like *jus d'orange* best."

"*De l'eau*," Paulette asks for more water for Mimi who is very thirsty and hungry after all that running, "*s'il vous plaît!*"

Sophie Starlette gives them cassettes of her songs and a picture of them all, then takes them home in her big car.

"*A bientôt*" she waves goodbye, "See you soon!"

Now it's eight o'clock and time for *le dîner*.
"I couldn't eat another thing," says Toto wearily.

It's very late when mum and dad arrive to take Toto back with them to the *hôtel*.
"*Bonne nuit, Paulette. Merci! Au revoir!*"

jus d'orange
joo d'orónj

pain au chocolat
pan oh shokolá

photo
fotóe

fourchette
foorshét

fromage
fromáj

couteau
kootóe

jouets jooáy

chat sha